This Ladybird Book belongs to:

_____

_____

_____

_____

This Ladybird retelling
by
Audrey Daly

Published by Ladybird Books Ltd
80 Strand London WC2R 0RL
A Penguin Company

11 13 15 17 19 20 18 16 14 12

© LADYBIRD BOOKS LTD 1993

Printed in Italy

FAVOURITE TALES

The Elves
and the
Shoemaker

illustrated
by
PETER STEVENSON

based on the story by Jacob and Wilhelm Grimm

Once upon a time there was a poor shoemaker who had no money left to buy food for himself and his wife. When he looked round his shop, he found that all he had was just enough leather to make one pair of shoes.

As he carefully cut out the shoes, he wondered sadly if anyone would ever come along to buy them. Then he laid out the leather on his workbench, ready to sew the next day, and went upstairs to bed.

In the morning, when he went to his workbench, the shoemaker couldn't believe his eyes. Instead of the leather he had cut out the night before, he saw a pair of fine shoes, already made.

The shoemaker looked carefully at the shoes. The stitches were small and even, and the shoes had been polished until they shone. He was very puzzled and showed them to his wife. Who could have made the shoes so perfectly?

Later that day, a rich woman came into the shop to buy some shoes. When the shoemaker showed her the pair he had found on his workbench, the woman smiled.

"These are very fine shoes," she said as she tried them on. "They fit perfectly. I'll give you five pieces of silver for them."

Now the shoemaker could buy some food, and he could also buy enough leather for *two* pairs of shoes.

As before, he cut out the leather and went to bed.

Once again, the same thing happened. When the shoemaker went to his workbench next day, there were two pairs of fine shoes waiting for him.

They were polished so that they glowed in the sunlight, and the stitches were small and even.

That afternoon, a rich merchant came into the shop. He liked the shoes so much that he bought *both* pairs, and he paid the shoemaker well for them.

That day, the shoemaker was able to buy enough leather for *four* pairs of shoes. Just as before, he cut out the leather and left it on his workbench overnight. And in the morning he found four fine pairs of shoes there instead.

The same thing happened night after night. And day after day, rich people came to buy the shoes. Soon the shoemaker and his wife were rich too.

One evening, not long before Christmas, the shoemaker said to his wife, "Someone has been helping us all this time, sewing the shoes so beautifully, and we still don't know who it is. How can we find out?"

"Well," said his wife, "why don't we stay up tonight and watch?"

So after dinner, they lit a candle and went into the shop. They hid behind the counter and waited to see what would happen.

At last the door opened and in ran two tiny elves, dressed in rags. They went straight to the workbench, picked up the leather lying there, and set to work.

They sewed and hammered until all
the shoes were finished. And they
polished every shoe until it shone in
the moonlight. Then they ran quickly
away.

The next morning, the shoemaker said to his wife, "Those elves have been working so hard for us. How can we ever repay them?"

"I know!" said his wife. "Why don't we make them something warm to wear? Their own clothes were thin and torn, and their little feet were bare. I could start by knitting them little caps, and you could make them some shoes."

The shoemaker thought that was a very good idea. That evening, he carefully made two pairs of tiny shoes, and his wife knitted two little caps.

Over the next few days, the shoemaker helped his wife to make all sorts of clothes for the elves. They made some little shirts, trousers and waistcoats. Finally, the shoemaker's wife knitted two tiny pairs of socks.

By Christmas Eve, everything stood ready in a little pile. The shoemaker's wife fetched some pretty paper and ribbons, and they wrapped each present one by one.

The shoemaker was so pleased with the little shoes he had made that he saved them till last, and wrapped them up very carefully.

Then they put all the presents out on the workbench, and hid behind the counter to wait for the elves.

In the middle of the night the elves dashed in, ready to start work. But when they went to the workbench, all they found there was the little pile of presents.

The elves looked at each other in surprise. Then they realised that the presents were for them, and they laughed and began to unwrap the packages.

When they saw the clothes, they leapt with joy. They took off all their ragged things and put on their brand new outfits.

Then the elves skipped merrily out of the door, singing,

*"Oh what handsome boys we are!
We will work on shoes no more!"*

That was the last the shoemaker and his wife saw of the two little men. But they never forgot the elves, and they were rich and happy for the rest of their lives.